Grandma, Does My Moon Shine Over Your House?

by *Mary Hansen Freund and Jane Freund*

Illustrated by Kristin Berkis Cottier

FREUNDSHIP PRESS

Positively influencing lives through friendship, communication, and education.

PO Box 9171
Boise, ID 83707
www.freundshippress.com
info@freundshippress.com

Positively influencing lives through friendship, communication, and education.

Freundship Press, LLC
PO Box 9171
Boise, ID 83707
(208) 407-7457
www.freundshippress.com
info@freundshippress.com

First printing 2010

ISBN-13: 978-1493762545 and ISBN-10: 1493762540

To order additional copies of this book, contact
Freundship Press as listed above.

To my grandchildren with love
from Grandma.
– *Mary Hansen Freund*

To Mom, congratulations
on being a published author and to
Kristin and Kris for helping to make
that dream possible.
– *Jane Freund*

To Brian, Bennett and Grayson,
thank you for your love and support,
and to Jane, thank you for
taking a chance.
– *Kristin Berkis Cottier*

Lynze was puzzled.

"What's wrong?" asked her Mom.

"I have a question for Grandma.
Can I call her?"
asked Lynze.

"Of course you may call Grandma.
I'll help you dial her number,"
offered her Mom.

"Hello," answered
a sweet voice.

"Grandma, I have a
question for you. . .

". . . Does my moon shine over your house?"

"Well Sweetie, there's only one moon.

So to answer your question, 'yes', your moon does shine over my house," replied Grandma.

"In fact, the moon travels across the entir

United States," added Grandma.

"That sounds like a tough job," exclaimed Lynze.

"I'm glad I'm not the moon!"

"Actually, Lynze, the moon takes about a month to travel around the whole world," explained Grandma.

"Wow, the moon must be so tired," replied Lynze.

"You're probably right," laughed Grandma.

18

"Thanks Grandma, I will think of you every time I see the moon," said Lynze.

"I love you,
Grandma."

"I love you too, Lynze,"
said Grandma.
"Bye now."

"So did Grandma answer your question?" asked Lynze's Mom.

"She sure did," answered Lynze. "I have the smartest Grandma in the whole world."

"Yes you do, Lynze, yes you do."

To order additional copies of "Grandma, Does My Moon Shine Over Your House?", please complete the order form below.

Name _____

Mailing Address _____

City _____

State_____ Zip _____

Phone Number(s) _____

Email _____

_____copy(ies) at $9.95 each for orders of 1-10 copies $ _____

_____copies at $8.95 each for orders over 10 copies $ _____

ID residents add 6% sales tax _____

Shipping and handling
(add $3.00 total for 1-10 copies OR FREE SHIPPING
for orders over 10 copies) _____

TOTAL DUE _____

Send check or money order (payable to Freundship Press, LLC) AND this order form to the following address:

> Freundship Press, LLC
> PO Box 9171
> Boise, ID 83707

If you have any questions, please e-mail info@freundshippress.com or phone (208) 407-7457.

To order using a credit or debit card, visit www.freundshippress.com

Mooser is on the loose in spring 2010!

Visit www.freundshippress.com for more details.

Positively influencing lives through friendship, communication, and education.

Made in the USA
Lexington, KY
01 December 2018